THE AUSTENITES

····································

Winner of the
SANDY RUN NOVELLA AWARD
From Hidden River Arts

····································

THE AUSTENITES

Beatriz Seelaender

HIDDEN RIVER PRESS

Philadelphia 2024

Cover Art: "Jane Austen's Home, Chawton, England" by Joe Giuffrida
Design and typography by P. M. Gordon Associates, Inc.

Library of Congress Control Number: 2022949582

ISBN 979-8-9854317-2-8

HIDDEN RIVER PRESS
An imprint of Hidden River Publishing
Philadelphia, Pennsylvania

*To my grandparents,
all four of them,
whose stories and histories
will always be important.*

One day . . . well, it doesn't matter why, but I was sitting in a gazebo, and there was a plaque on the gazebo and it said, 'This gazebo was built by the town in 1863'. That is in the middle of the Civil War. And the whole town built a gazebo. What was that town meeting like? 'All right, everyone, first order of business, we have all the telegrams from Gettysburg with the war dead. Let's see here. Okay, everyone's husband and brother and . . . everyone died. Okay. Josiah, you had something?' 'Yes, I do. How'd you like to be indoors and out of doors all at once? Ever walk into the park with your betrothed and it starts to rain, but you still want to hold hands? Well, may I introduce you to, and my condolences again to everyone, the gazebo!'

—JOHN MULANEY

Contents

THE AUSTENITES

Saving Jane

It is a truth universally acknowledged that one can no longer, out of his own ethical duty towards philosophical enlightenment, acknowledge the existence of any universal truths. That was how Major Elias McBride, of His Majesty's Fifth Regiment, saw the world—a bent, blood-sucking leech, not turning but bending, and he knows he already said bending but that's how it is; the world.

Before one spends too long dwelling on his backstory, Major McBride is willing to share one or two details about himself. a) He is a Scotsman first, everything else second. b) Even though he's been stationed at Chawton for the rest of the war, the war is so long he'll never rest; he wishes he could go back to the line of combat. c) He's really not one of those arseholes who gets something out of war, a sick thrill like some of them do about dying and sacrificing themselves; but he'd also like to do more than teach civilians about evacuation. d) It's not that he doesn't think it's necessary or important to teach people about those things, but his training included more than giving out instructions. e) Only they won't let him back into the front, since his leg has been blown into threads of bone, glued back together like some delicate statue made out of flower stems. f) There are bombings constantly. He is so damn tired of these bloody bombings and those bloody Nazis thinking they can just do whatever to them. Oh, the year is 1944. Things might be starting to look up for Britain, but do not look up just yet—there'll be a plane carrying a bomb. And looking up will only have you paralysed.

Here's the thing about this war, he thinks: even if we win, we lose. The whole place has been blown to bits! We've been fighting our arses off for five years, and only now do the Americans bother showing up. And who do you think is going to get the most out of it? Who do you think is going to get the parades and the glory? We, who've been going head-to-head with little shithead Adolf since the beginning, or the opportunistic Americans? That, provided we actually beat Adolf. People come up to me and say, *I know So-and-So who's at the front—do you know him?* Why would I know him? Everybody's got a So-and-So in the front; you can't bloody know them all. It's not bloody Ascot, you're not betting on horses. It's not like I've been summering at the war—*Oh, The War, you say? You've never been?* Ha! And what do we do when the war is over? Reconstruct? Go back to our lives, try to regain a sense of normalcy? This war is never going to be over. This war is what the rest of our lives will be like. It's just the times. Bad times. Bad timing to be born, to be fit to fight—better to be sick and frail. All of those children born during the last war, already orphaned, who have to go fight this one now. Why even bother being someone? Becoming someone, that is. You're just going to be a soldier.

A knock on the door interrupts his imaginary conversation—it's his superior, Lieutenant Colonel Hendricks, who seems a fussy man, from a distance.

"Sir," greeted Elias, "Do you need me?"

"Not immediately, no. I just want to inform you that I have found something else for you to do—that is, if you are really discontent with the evacuation training. I realize anyone could do *that*. This new duty is more of a National Service task."

"Yes, sir, I'd be honoured."

"Good! In that case, I'd like to introduce you to Lady Durrell of Saint Augustine's College for Girls."

Lady Durrell was then pulled into the room by the fussy man. It was clear she'd been standing just outside the whole time. It was horridly theatrical, and something so pathetic as that, at a time like this, seemed to Elias to be profoundly distasteful. But Lady Durrell herself did not seem distasteful—her black hair was pulled back in a business-like manner, she wore a coat both sober and majestic, and her high cheekbones did the work of distancing herself from Colonel Hendricks' oddball movements.

"How do you do?" she said, distractedly, and did not leave much room for an answer as she shook Elias's hand, "Professor Mabel Durrell, wonderful to meet you."

She had yet to learn his name.

"Likewise," he said, offering her a chair.

"What I have to discuss with you, sir, is a matter of international proportions."

"Yes?"

"As both of you gentlemen probably know, this town Chawton harbours Jane Austen's brother's house, Chawton House. I mean, obviously. It would be quite absurd if Chawton House were located anywhere else."

Both gentlemen nodded, accepting the information as commonplace. They did not want to appear uncultured.

"Anyhow, given the more-than-frequent bombings that this region has been suffering, it has dawned upon me and some other scholars that an Elizabethan Mansion with which Jane Austen had a personal connection may be in danger of permanent damage. We've been raising money for such causes ever since the beginning of the war—we've funded the same sort of protection for the British Museum, the British Library, the National Gallery. . . . These places must be protected from bombings and such. In Chawton House's case, we funded a trust and, with government help, have decided to fortify the structure of the building."

"Your ladyship has raised money for all that?" asked the colonel.

"Well, I did not do it alone. Many people have contributed. This is not official MFAA business, but it is supported by them."

"MFAA?"

"The Monuments, Fine Arts, and Achievements? The Allies' program to protect cultural heritage? I volunteer for them."

"Marvellous!" he said, "Splendid! Major McBride is at your ladyship's services."

"That is very generous of you both, gentlemen. I do need an army-man with knowledge of German bombs—someone who's actually been out of the bubble. Granted, it's not a very fortified bubble, but a bubble nonetheless. I wish nations could just fight without destroying any historical heritage."

And, with that sharp observation, Professor Durrell said her goodbyes and expressed her pleasure at working with Major McBride, whose name she still had not bothered asking. Major McBride was not pleased:

"All due respect, Colonel, I requested a job that made more of a difference, not one that is even more isolating."

"This is an important project, Major."

"Protecting a building that no one lives in? That only goes to show rich people would rather have people die than lose one of their mansions!"

"Let us not point fingers. Chawton Mansion is an important patrimony for British history. Lady Durrell has her scholarly hobbies; it is important to her to feel like she's doing something— as it is to you, major."

"So, I get to feel useful by making Lady Durrell feel useful even though she's chosen to feed into her posh oblivion instead of helping actual people in need?"

Colonel Hendricks shrugged. He thought it was quite lovely an assignment—much better than assigning people to go to the front, which was his own particular duty.

Major Elias McBride hadn't much in his possession other than assorted memories he carried around. He'd been the second-born son in his family, and had to learn how to fend for himself from a young age. His father, a useless blue blood who thought work too demeaning, spent up to his last penny trying to keep up appearances and refusing to entertain the bourgeoisie.

The older Mr. McBride had been an arduous supporter of the Empire, and personally donated money to smother any Scottish Independence Movement that had ever arisen, which earned him praise from the King's public relations.

However controversial a figure Mr. McBride might have been, Elias did get a sense of nostalgia out of missing him—he may have left both his sons penniless and unprepared to deal with the ways of the world, but the world that he had lived in was so much simpler. It was uncanny, disorienting even, just how much had changed. Even if Mr. McBride had cared to prepare his children to enter the real world back then, Elias doubted they'd ever have been able to put it into practice. No, back then he leapt through the green sheets of the forests of the Highlands, hopped through stones that paved bridges between riverbanks; he watched sheep herders from afar and got his hands dirty from playing in the fresh land of the farm, the land that grew everything: vegetables and grains and boys—very young boys like himself growing out of the shiny grainy optimal land. That was the earth; one could always dig deeper, and it brought great amounts of joy to him when he was a child. Oh, Scotland, his native heart. It was a pit in his stomach, a deep well in his gut that pulled him toward the land. He could still taste the planted seeds in the dirt he ate so much of as a child, there on his tongue.

He arrived at Chawton House that morning not knowing what to expect. It was a beautiful place, and the existence of beautiful places in times such as these seemed terribly incongruous to him. Elias felt both guilty and offended by Chawton's unbothered greenery. Lady Durrell and her aristocratic minions emerged from her motorised carriage before he could get a good look around the gardens.

Lady Durrell wore a fashionable coat, cut into precision; and her cheekbones seemed even higher in that outfit than before, which made her frame both aesthetically pleasing and rather statuesque. So much, in fact, that Durrell's crew—which included one architect called Mercer, a friend Lady Corey, and an older, grave-looking woman—seemed dour and dire in comparison.

Upon that thought, Elias must have smiled widely, which caused one of the women to ask him what was so funny.

"Oh, nothing much. I've just, you know, never been here."

"Inside?"

"Yeah."

"It is quite lovely, isn't it? It would be a shame if it all went to pieces."

"Yes, indeed."

The man called Mercer intercepted the conversation:

"You have been abroad lately, haven't you, Major?"

"At the front, sir, you mean?"

"Yes, precisely."

"I have, sir."

"Have you witnessed many bombings? In Germany, Austria, etc? Are the buildings still standing there? Such marvellous buildings! Just think of how long it will be to rebuild everything from the ground!"

"Well, one must fight fire with fire, I suppose," said Elias, a bit annoyed already at his inverted priorities.

"I suppose," agreed Mercer, though his eyes seemed to wander off.

"I mean," Elias went on, "They are just buildings."

Mercer now held a murderous expression behind his eyes. The old woman, Professor Franklin, interfered with a smile, "Mr. Mercer is genuinely hurt over those buildings, yes. Now, James, that might make you seem unpatriotic to our new friend. Major McBride, however poorly Mercer expresses himself, he has been serving the army by designing underground shelters, bunkers, and all sorts of patriotic spaces."

"I am not a patriot myself, Professor Franklin. I believe Patriotism leads to the sort of atrocity we are suffering today. There is nothing that ties me to Britain's cause other than this country is on the right side of things. At least where the war is concerned. Which is why I and, I believe, Mr. Mercer—who, of course, has probably helped this country in a greater scale than I could ever dream of—fight our daily fights," said Elias, smiling again. That brought Mercer back into the conversation.

"Well, I will not boast about it, of course. There is no beauty in it. No time for beauty. I personally do not care for the work of Marinetti, saying that art and war work are alike—that one needs the other. War gets in the way of art and runs over it. It's all such a shame, really. See, buildings—buildings are like lobsters."

"Pardon me, sir?"

"Like lobsters—lobsters do not die until they are killed."

"I should imagine!"

The ladies laughed.

"No, no," said Mr. Mercer in all seriousness, "Unless we kill them, lobsters do not die."

"Are you quite certain of that, Mr. Mercer?" asked Professor Franklin, "It seems like—forgive me—poppycock."

"It's the truth! Apparently, they do not age."

"Do they not age, or do they not die?"

"I . . . If you did not like my metaphor, Professor Franklin, I'll think of another. My point is that buildings survive us all. Buildings . . ."

It sounded as if he were about to start a pompous praise of Architecture.

"No, calm down. One cannot afford such sentimentality in times like these," said Lady Durrell, speaking for the first time. She had, while the others talked, been inspecting the fissures in the walls.

"I don't think the Army can spare an engineer right now, Mr. Mercer, so would you care to have a look at those? Perhaps determine whether you could fix them?"

"It would be my utmost pleasure, Lady Durrell."

Even though Mercer seemed at least a foot taller than Durrell, he seemed to fall at her feet. His expression deteriorated into a servile nod as he went to examine the site.

"Now, Major McBride, would you mind inspecting the gardens with me?"

"Of course, Professor."

The gardens at Chawton Manor, despite being mildly cared for, remained a bit too wild for someone as snobbish as Mabel Durrell. She moved, attempting to avoid every twig out of place and every water puddle that threatened her shoes. It was a serpentine, reptile-like dance she did with the vegetation, a game she played to see how long until the tree's elongated fingers touched her.

"So, you don't care for buildings?" She threw him a long, patronising look, and didn't even bother to hide her mocking smile.

"I enjoy looking at them. I'm not entirely sure whether we should prioritize them over people."

"I don't much care for buildings either, actually. I do care about this building, though."

"It is beautiful, I'll give you that."

She smiled poorly, again.

"It's really about Jane Austen," she said in a matter-of-fact way, as if he were daft.

"Oh. I don't care much for her, either."

"Have you ever read her, Major McBride?"

"Somewhat."

"Somewhat?"

"Bits and pieces."

"Right. You do understand, then, Major, why I must ask you to familiarise yourself with her before we start this endeavour?"

"Is this a reading assignment?"

"Somewhat. You see, I fear that you, sir, will not grasp the importance of this mission unless you understand what Austen means to our culture. And, by not grasping it, you will find my efforts not only unnecessary but, at a time like this, also insulting to our people."

"You make a good point, Professor."

"Of course, people are capable of protecting themselves. And there is also the Army, and the government, to protect them. I wish I could protect everyone, but this money that has been raised specifically to protect Austen's house, in all truth, would make little to no difference in the grand scheme of things. War-wise, I mean. By protecting this house, however, the money will go into something manageable."

"If you permit me saying this, Professor, it seems as though the person you are trying to convince is not me but yourself."

"I am not delusional. I know it seems superfluous. But in reality art is what holds us together. Literature, architecture, music . . . That is what makes us human. If we lose that, then all we are left with is—well—a numbness of spirit. A refusal to engage . . . So much directionless rage, a rage that gives up on one's sense of self, turns one into a weapon of hatred . . . Art *gives* one a sense of self. Reading, especially, is a lot like seeing through a mirror—it is confirmation of an inner-life, one's own inner-life, different from everyone else's. It's proof that we are real even in fiction—that we are responsive and subjective. That we are more than our place and time."

Was she still talking to him? She seemed a bit surprised by the length of her own monologue. When she started, she intended to just make herself clear once and for all. But he kept on looking at her judgementally—yes, he was judgemental. And so she had responded to his challenges until her rhetoric started faltering.

"If a human being," she continued, "does not know art, he no longer knows how to think or feel. It doesn't matter that all he does is think. He is thinking someone else's thoughts. He's feeling someone else's feelings, their idea of how they should feel. We need to work on preventing that vacancy of mind in Britain. It is precisely what drove the Germans into gore—lack of empathy, lack of reflection. There's just so much that's wrong, you see? You may think literature is a frivolous thing to be worried about, but it is the most *fundamental* aspect of humanity . . . This whole capitalist enterprise has clouded our minds into thinking that things only matter when they provide us with immediate compensation. Knowledge without an aim? Knowledge for the sake of knowing? God save us from actually valuing information that does not go towards our pockets but our spirits!"

"Professor Durrell, I understand what you are saying, yes, but do you understand that your dismissiveness towards money could be linked to the fact that you are in possession of an abundance of it?"

She laughed—though not mockingly this time.

"Oh, I understand that perfectly, Major. Now I'll leave you to inspect the area. By Tuesday, I expect you to have finished at least one novel by Jane Austen."

Mabel Durrell refused to be referred to as a "Janeite". The term had been coined by academics as a derogatory way to address the Jane Austen reader who was not an academic. The common assumption was that reading Austen's works counted for very little if one was reading them inadequately. Reading a work of art is nothing unless one reads it well. Mabel was certain that the only reason she did not like certain classics was that she had not read them well. But to read well is to read deeply and alone, and it was the same as to think by oneself. There is no one interpretation of a book just as there is no one interpretation of a person. You have conversations with them, and you either like or dislike them. You either understand or not. But you must always try to understand.

She knew not why she cared so much about these issues—they kept her up at night the same way the usual questions (one's own mortality, the existence of one or more supreme deities, how people actually are as opposed to how we perceive them or if there's any difference in the end—fine, she worried about those as well, though not nearly as much), tormented others. In any case, she was terrified of committing a reading blunder, and there was no greater one than being a Janeite.

The Janeite, it was determined, was simply a mindless idiot who got into Jane Austen for all of the wrong reasons—namely, the love stories. The ideal Austen reader dismissed those as bait to get the masses invested. The love stories were there simply to mask sharp social critique as an innocent, feminine affectation—like medicine artificially flavoured to trick children into taking it—indeed does a spoon full of sugar make the medicine go down.

The real Austen reader, however—the Austenite—would take the antibiotics in flavourless pills, thank you very much. Where a Janeite would swoon, a scholar would snort, vividly—even if he or she were the only ones in the room, because their scientific soberness required a daily care routine. No, she was an Austenite, not a Janeite.

Where one found a Janeite waiting for her Mr. Darcy, right behind her one was sure to find a brave Austenite disclaiming Austen's notions on love and marriage as a product of the growing bourgeois social establishment. It was as if an alarm set off every time a Janeite found any pleasure in an Austen novel, so the nearest Austenite could be summoned to explain to her what it was *really* about. It does not matter that scholars are greatly outnumbered by misinformed Janeites—they will show up to explain that Jane Austen is not for your enjoyment, but for your instruction, young lady.

Most importantly, the real Jane Austen reader, though cautiously appreciative of *Pride and Prejudice*, found that Austen only reached her full potential when she wrote *Persuasion*.

Mabel, however, did not care much for *Persuasion*—she found it unfunny. In reality, her favourite Austen book would always be *Emma*, which was not necessarily a popular choice among her group—the eponymous character, as Mr. Mercer had put it, was simply too vicious for anyone to care about her woes— but the novel was still acceptable because it wasn't much of a love story, either.

It was also the first Jane Austen novel she had ever read— and there was something about discovering an author; the book that leads one to a body of work is always closer to the soul. Mabel wondered which novel Major McBride would choose— it would probably be *Pride and Prejudice*. It was the one most people started with—hence, the distasteful cult surrounding it.

Later that evening as Mabel Durrell's group drove away; they each had a different opinion of Major McBride:

"He's quite fluent at expressing his opinions," said Mr. Mercer, "for a man of his rank and file. One would think he was born into money. That, or very generous masters."

"I suppose he found it ludicrous that we wanted to preserve something simply because of a connection it has with Miss Austen," said Lady Corey, who always referred to Jane Austen as such.

"He did not find it ludicrous, Arabella. He found it wrong," said Mabel, looking away through the window of the passenger seat. "He may have picked up some bits of culture here and there, and he is clever, he speaks well. But McBride is a man of the world; he is in the end as simple—and narrow-minded—as any soldier."

"You spoke to him?" asked the older lady, Professor Franklin.

"Briefly. He said he had read Austen *somewhat*. How does one *somewhat* read something?"

"Well, you know; bits and pieces," said Arabella.

"That is hardly the right way to read anything."

"My dearest Mabel, does he actually irritate you?" asked Mercer.

"As much as any other uncultured swine, I suppose."

Professor Franklin interjected: "God, Mabel, do you hear yourself speak sometimes? You should. You sound like a spoilt brat."

Mabel did not pay attention to those remarks. "Although, perhaps his insolence makes me despise him more. How dare he accuse me of being superfluous?"

"He actually said that?"

"Well, in a way. He said something like it."

"I see. Do you want us to find another army-man?" asked Mercer.

"No, don't be ridiculous. I am capable of working with people I dislike."

After that, no one said anything until they reached the road, though the consensus seemed to be that a) Mabel's statement was probably true because b) there weren't many people whom Mabel actually liked. That is, apart from characters in novels.

Lady Durrell had always loved reading more than she loved living, not only because books skipped to the interesting parts, but because reading was the only ritual that had forged her own individuality all the while allowing her to be a thousand different variations of herself. To her, art was freedom, albeit of a vicarious sort, and distant. Mabel liked to think anyone who had a vivid imaginative life would always be free, no matter how trying the circumstances.

Literature allows the reader to be and not to be at the same time, to connect with others and yet to be completely and utterly alone simultaneously. She often reflected, in fact, that only when she was alone could she be herself, nameless and whole. Or maybe that was her letting go of herself. Come to think of it, it was probably both.

All this talk of war; this concern only with urgent matters, was bound to have dreadful consequences: the world, as Walter Benjamin had observed, would always be on the brink of chaos. Contemporary society's natural state was a state of emergency. People like Major McBride were doubtless fit to put out the fire in the curtains, while she would search for the source of it.

The idea that culture should not be prioritised in times such as these is why this happened in the first place. The group ideology of Nazi-Fascism happened only because no one had done enough reading and visiting of museums. Had they experienced art properly, they would have come in contact with their own inevitable individuality instead of renouncing it for some idiotic notion such as patriotism.

It was a pity, given German and Italian intellectual and artistic traditions, but now the brutality of group ideology had contaminated their society: Deny your own self; it's easy to start denying others that same privilege. Only bodies, bundled up cold and dirty and disgusting.

Yet that was all people cared about: bodies. Mabel scarcely remembered she had one. In her view, her mortal frame was simply a vessel for her immortal mind. She would much rather live in a country filled with starving artists than one of sufficiently fed philistines.

Elias was, in some ways, ashamed of going to a bookshop at times like these. Leisure seemed irresponsible, even if it was theoretically commissioned by the Ministry of Defence. He was also ashamed—though he was redeemably ashamed to admit this as well—of buying Jane Austen books, who he had consciously avoided throughout his life due to the impression they were all sappy romance novels written for spinsters, widows, and young girls who enjoy fantasy and escapism.

He picked the first Austen book he could find, which was *Mansfield Park*. He read it reluctantly, getting up and down to check on his tea kettle. He did not really take pleasure in it—mainly, it was an issue with focusing, but it was also that the protagonist Fanny was a bit of a dimwit.

When he shared his thoughts with Professor Durrell later in the week, she looked at him as if he were an untrained monkey. Rolling her eyes, she said he should never have started with *Mansfield Park* because *Mansfield Park* was an utter bore of a book. She did not know why Austen had written it in the first place. Then she gave Elias a copy of *Sense and Sensibility* that she seemed to just be carrying around with her.

"You can have it," she said of him and the copy, though looking at neither directly, "I have loads of those around the house."

He took the book. She had scribbled mindlessly all through the margins.

"What, are you complaining?" she asked when she noticed he was still there. "You're lucky to have those notes. They're illuminating! Better than any Cambridge Companion. Assuming you can read them, of course."

"I can read, Professor, obviously."

"Well, how should I know? You seem so dumbstruck."

"All due respect, Lady Durrell, that was highly disrespectful; and it is not my job to serve as punching bag. If that is in fact what you want, you shall sacrifice another soldier to your noble cause, as I'm sure to find someone who takes twisted pleasure in following orders without question."

Her face contorted into an expression of rage. She took a deep breath. "You are right. I'm sorry. You see, you've caught me on a very stressful day and I have been known to lash out at those who've been nothing but kind to me. Please, forgive me for my mindless rudeness."

"Of course," Elias accepted. He could tell the Professor wanted him to apologise, too, for his irritating attitude, or at least issue a lengthier forgiveness, but he did not want to say anything more about it, at risk of saying something that might continue an already unpleasant conversation.

Elias let the silence resound for one more moment and then proceeded. "I'm not an idiot, you know, Professor."

"Oh, I know that."

"I don't know that you do. Some of us actually have put some effort into getting proper instruction, and you should trust that I have. I don't dismiss cultural activities. I simply believe using Culture as a way to escape reality is unproductive."

"I don't use Culture as a way to escape. I use it as a way to understand."

"I'm afraid there are some things you just can't understand unless you've actually lived through them."

"Yes, sir, you are probably right. Colonel Hendricks told me what happened to your leg. I'm terribly sorry."

"I wasn't talking about my leg. Although living my life as a cripple isn't half as redemptive as your beloved novels would lead one to believe. No, I was talking about the sheer hypocrisy of it all. How artificial our lives are."

"Oh, that. I think that once you get the hang of Austen, you'll be good friends."

"Up until now, all that I got was the surly moral judgement of a resentful main character."

"But that is *Mansfield Park*. God only knows what was going through Austen's head. Moral judgements here and there, the unconventional heroine—Miss Crawford, of course, being much more of the traditional Austen protagonist, and not *idiotic* Fanny. Some will tell you Mansfield Park is Austen's best book, but those are people whose bad taste extends everywhere else."

"You have very strong feelings about this."

She took offense in that. "Oh, you intend to say I have very strong feelings about unimportant things such as—it is implied—Jane Austen. Don't worry, Major, I can hear myself perfectly. Call me an elitist if you like, I will not let this war dictate my every thought. Austen may not be urgent, but she is necessary. Like Shakespeare—only more so, because Shakespeare is so idolized I find myself growing tired of him."

He pictured Lady Durrell tossing aside a copy of King Lear, saying "I love Your Majesty according to my bond, no more nor less", then laughing at her own joke. He had played Cordelia in a boarding school play, making her lines the only Shakespeare he knew by heart.

"That is a bold statement," he remarked.

"Laugh all you want, Major McBride. Books are important—have you ever heard that story about that Portuguese epic poet?"

"I am ashamed to confess I have never heard of any Portuguese epic poet."

"Camões was his name. He wrote about the great sea expeditions extensively; certainly he would have been more successful had he spoken another language—then again, it was the historic concern of his nation. Anyhow, there is a story—I don't know whether it's true, though I'd rather believe in it. It is said Camões and his betrothed—who couldn't swim, such an irresponsible thing to travel by sea if one cannot swim—were aboard a ship when it started to sink. He had to make a choice: save her, or the manuscript he'd just finished."

"I suppose he chose the manuscript?" guessed Elias, expecting some absurd moral to the story.

"Which went on to become the most important epic poem of the Portuguese language, *The Lusiads*."

"In conclusion, we must sacrifice a few brides-to-be in the name of Literature," he proclaimed sarcastically.

Not exactly, thought Mabel—if the lady had managed to survive the shipwreck, she doubted she would still want to be Camões' bride. She kept herself from correcting him, however, as the matter was petty.

"Suppose he'd saved her—she might have gone on to live a few decades longer. The poem, on the other hand, is almost four hundred years old," she argued. It had a much greater life than the person who died."

A greater shelf life, perhaps. The most frivolous question wandered into his head: how had the manuscript remained dry? Even if it was in a box or something similar, surely it would have taken in water.

"As long as that's the lesson . . . Manuscripts and children first," Elias mocked. "Suppose the Germans set fire to the Louvre. Should the *Mona Lisa* be the first one rescued given her greater life expectancy?"

"Don't be absurd—there are far better paintings in the Louvre than the *Mona Lisa*," she smiled slyly.

"Now, you're not being quite serious, Lady Durrell?"

She shrugged, a gesture mightily inappropriate for a lady, according to her former governess. She had also never read a word of Camões.

"The point is," she said, though she now forgot what her point had been. Something about the legacy of art. Yes, that was it: "Books and buildings and pictures and plays live longer than people. That's fine—they were made to that purpose of outliving us all. We owe it that much to the people who came before to preserve them," she professed. "After all is said and done, this war isn't just killing the living; it is killing the legacy of the dead. Right now it's simply collateral damage; to future historians it will be their lament in every study. *Somebody* has to care."

In that, she had a point: books being burned by Nazis, Nazis stealing and sacking and looting. Buildings that had managed to stay up for centuries blown up in seconds. Elias had seen it all with alarming apathy. But he also knew their present efforts, which already counted for very little, would count for nothing in the long run if rich people continued to misspend their money on futile endeavours.

"Lady Durrell, perhaps you are right. And perhaps you are indeed destined to be the saviour of long-dead artists. But there's no point to doing any of this if we lose the war."

Lady Durrell gave a crooked smile which, he found, suited her face .

"We aren't going to lose the war," she said.

"How can you be so sure?"

"It just wouldn't make sense."

The Major thought that, if a requirement for reality was for things to make sense, then this war wouldn't have been happening in the first place. But of course Mabel Durrell still believed in the orderly aspect of the universe.

"What do you mean by that?" he pushed her for more clarity.

"Do you believe in God, Major?"

God? Where had that come from? The Major had assumed Lady Durrell, like most educated people, was in the process of easing Him out of the conversation. Order? Yes. God? No. God was a former nobleman forced to surrender His assets. Although He was still tolerated in the circles in which He used to run, there was a great unease whenever He entered a room. Instead of subjecting themselves to the awkwardness of asking Him to leave, his friends would instead faze Him out and ignore Him. But Lady Durrell was pointing at the ghost of God now and asking Elias if he saw it, too.

"Not particularly. I mean . . . No, I don't," he answered, a bit ashamed.

"Me neither. I believe the idea of a god essential for men to become civilized. But once they are civilized, believing in God seems quite irrational and primitive. Of course, not believing in God seems quite presumptuous."

That Lady Durrell would ever worry about sounding presumptuous came as a shock to Elias.

"All I know is that God-fearing men may well be dangerous, but those who found something else entirely to believe in are more difficult to contain. Especially when that "thing" believed in is merely themselves."

That, Elias found, he must agree with.

"But you said we would win the war. How does God help us win the war?"

Lady Durrell tilted her head, and smiled as if she were about to say something extremely stupid, which she was aware was extremely stupid, proving she was not herself stupid.

"Not necessarily God. Just . . . narrative coherence: in a narrative, it's always one step forward, two steps back. But you can't take three steps back, you know what I mean? You can't, otherwise it's just . . ."

"Not realistic?" He understood. It was an irrational sentiment, but much stupider things had been said, some of them by her, some of them only moments ago.

"You've got to have a win," she continued. "You need to take some cold comfort in the thought that, even though the world is mostly terrible, it is never as terrible as it could have been. But, if we lose this war . . ."

She got quiet and sombre. Elias understood that particular alignment of wrinkles, even if it made no sense drafted upon a Lady's face. He too was haunted by a dreadful mass in the pit of his stomach; it kept him from the world, down the rabbit hole into the earth's teeth. It pulled him into the dirt, down every well, into the earth's very stomach, through its thick skin of stones made out of carcasses and magma.

His leg hurt, the lack thereof. The one he'd lost somewhere in France—he could feel it rotting still; he was there and the leg was gangrene and the leg was gone. Shards of bullets and bombs going off without a care in the world.

Elias pulled himself back, forcing himself to speak. "It's a lie, that things aren't always as bad as they seem. Sometimes, bad's all there is. I understand that. I've heard of things that have made me wish—I, an atheist who despises the idea of the afterlife—they have made me wish I were wrong and there really were a Hell, just so those bloody Nazis could get their share."

"That is very poetic of you," she said mockingly.

He had obviously misread her expression, he now realized. Perhaps he'd hurdled one too many nightmares lately and was desperate for a confidant. How silly of him, to think of Lady Durrell as such!

Major McBride, oftentimes, felt himself so prone to errors of judgement, virulent attacks, night-terrors. As much as he liked to think himself a strong man, the best he could wish for now was that others maintain that opinion of him even when he could not. There had been tales of men who'd been turned into shells by war; Elias could only hope to withstand that kind of fate with determined resilience. Deep down inside he still felt exposed to every threat; his armour was no shell; it was a shallow peel.

The Intellectual During Wartime

~

Mr. James Elliot Mercer, PhD, had gone to Oxford at the promising age of eighteen and left at the more sober age of four-and-twenty. While Architecture was his true passion, he had been known to dabble in the realms of High Literature, and his interest in Jane Austen—whose work he saw as Medium Literature at best—he had developed as a hobby. Mr. Mercer found playing cards to be growing ever-demeaning for a man of his rank and file, and just as his losses started to outweigh the profit, Mr. Mercer decided to take on a new distraction—something that was based on cleverness rather than sheer dumb luck. It was also auspicious that the object of his affection, Lady Mabel Sienna Durrell, was invested in a Jane-Austen-related project.

There were some things about Mabel of which even Mercer did not approve. Her combative spirit and assertive way of speaking were hardly attractive qualities in anyone. All that he wanted was for Lady Durrell to smile at him, once a day—for her smile was like the Sun to him, and everything good in the world perished in darkness when she didn't smile. It was possible that her spinster friends—Professor Franklin especially—had been putting ideas into her head, about how women become weak when they marry. But Mr. Mercer was working on changing her mind about that, and volunteering himself for her projects was a big part of it.

He had considered sending Professor Franklin off to teach in America, where she—as a Jewish person—would be safer, and he would be safe from the influence she exerted over Lady Durrell. He needed to go about it very carefully, though, so that she wouldn't suspect he wanted her gone. He would plant the idea in her mind, or speak to his classmate from Eton who now taught in some New Jersey suburb. Once he got rid of Professor Franklin's bad influence on Mabel, he could initiate a proper wooing process. Who wouldn't want to live in the same house as his magnificent library? He'd recently picked up the habit of collecting rare manuscripts; it seemed that everyone was selling them at a bargain. Professor Franklin suggested that they had come from dubious sources, but Mercer refused to believe that. The people he with whom he conducted business were serious about their trade. Besides, Professor Franklin had told them all many unbelievable stories about what was going on in her native Germany.

Not that he didn't like Professor Franklin—she was an educated woman, even by a man's standards. As he had told her many times already, she might as well be a man. What an eccentric little creature! She sat with men at faculty gatherings, playing cards, smoking cigars, laughing at men's jokes. Although, to be fair, one must act like a man in order to be able to think as clearly as one. Some would go as far as to say that she had pursued relationships with women. Homoerotic relations, that is.

Yes, Mr. Mercer found that to be in poor taste, but he was will-ing to excuse certain instances of moral misconduct if they led to academic breakthroughs—and Professor Franklin, though peculiar, was the closest thing to a male brain those women at St. Augustine had.

Of course, there was the issue with the dress code—he'd never even seen her wear a dress; not even a skirt. Professor Franklin had an exclusive relationship with trousers. He suspected she—on top of being a lesbian—might be a crossdresser, but could not bring himself to share that suspicion with anyone. So poor Mr. Mercer simply resigned himself to these private thoughts—he was prepared to tolerate her being in the same party as him and to swallow his concerns, if not for academic open-mindedness, for dearest Lady Durrell.

"It might be," Professor Franklin was saying, "that our society's notions of *Culture* are alienating."

They were all spread, slightly, on a Persian carpet that looked frigidly out of place in a dusty living room under renovation. Because they had all needed a break, Elias had made them tea. And now they sat in awkward positions as they sipped from their cups.

Lady Corey, who seemed second in ceremonious display only to Mr. Mercer, was still standing up, to avoid any assumptions about her reputation. Professor Franklin and the men had the advantage of pants, though Mr. Mercer seemed utterly uncom-fortable trying to cross his legs.

"Oh, spare me, Esther," Lady Durrell said.

" You are aware of how much I both admire and respect you, Professor Franklin, but we need only look to find hundreds of books at our disposal at one's local public library," said Mr. Mer-cer, happy to disagree.

"That isn't the whole story. Culture is used as a tool by peo-ple like us, James, in order to oppress people with fewer means."

"Nonsense! Forgive me, Professor, but that is absurd," protested Mercer.

"No, I do think you have a point, Esther," said Mabel, "Culture *is* alienating and information is voluntarily kept from the lower classes. *That* I agree with. I have a problem with what you were going to say afterword."

"Oh, really, Mabel, you know what I was going to say even before I did?"

"You're not exactly subtle. You were going to tell us that, because of how alienating *Culture*—with a capital C—is, because of how unachievable it may seem to the masses, it should be undermined. You were going to say we need lower our standards instead of raising those of the ignorant portions of the population, which is ridiculous."

"Well, I wouldn't have phrased it like that, no. I was just wondering why what we consider culture is considered better than, say, low literature . . . Like detective stories," said Professor Franklin.

"Detective stories? They just give you the answer!", said Mr. Mercer.

"I enjoy a good detective story every now and then," said Lady Corey.

"I don't think it is necessarily low. Only because something is easier to understand, that doesn't make it worse," that was Elias speaking from the corner of the room.

Everyone on the carpet looked at him:

"Do you like detective stories, Major McBride?" asked Mabel.

"Sometimes," he said, worried he'd made a fool of himself. "You know, Sir Arthur Conan Doyle, Jack London . . . Stories that go . . . beyond?"

Apparently he'd said what Lady Durrell had wished of him, because she turned her head back, triumphantly:

"He means that some stories, regardless of form, are able to transcend certain limitations imposed to them. And you're right, Major. *Anyone* who's read Kant and Hegel can draw the same conclusion. Just because something is enjoyable it does not mean it is aesthetically enjoyable—on the contrary, the aesthetics of our last artistic movements have been quite disruptive. And not only in Literature—think of Schiele! God, think of abstract art!"

"I would rather not," joked Mr. Mercer, and that did get him some laughs. But Mabel was impatient to make her point:

"What I'm saying, of course, is that art reflects the thought and spirit—and soul—of man. And that it can be just about anything, apart from that whose sole purpose is either to be art or to not be art."

"Oh, Mabel, stop for a second there. You are building a thesis over tea. It is much appreciated, but perhaps you'd like to write this down and tell us later," said Mr. Mercer.

She looked at Elias:

"See, Major, Mr. Mercer here simply hates being around people who might express intelligent thoughts around him, thoughts that have not yet occurred to him."

"Lady Durrell—that is not true!"

"It's all right, Mr. Mercer. I'm only teasing you. Of course that it isn't true, otherwise you could not get out of the house as much as you do."

Professor Franklin snorted on her tea.

"Lady Durrell, that is hardly nice of you," Mr. Mercer sounded deeply hurt.

"I'm joking, Mr. Mercer, I told you."

"Even so. You could be nicer."

Mabel tilted her head and, as if she'd just stopped to reflect on it, said with mild surprise, "I don't think I could. I'm afraid I'm not a very nice person."

Professor Franklin and Lady Corey burst out laughing.

"Nonsense! You're delightful!" said Mercer, contradicting himself in his haste to praise. Mabel turned to Elias:

"What do you think, Major McBride? You've only just met me—would you say I'm nice? Be honest."

"I think you are a highly intelligent woman," answered the major, "whose Culture I deeply admire."

"But I'm not nice," concluded Mabel, and Elias could detect a hint of pride in her voice. That is, on top of the usual amount.

She seemed entertained by the situation she'd put him in, like she was challenging him. Right now, Elias wanted to leave and never have to look at Lady Durrell's face again.

"God, no," he said, which led to some unrequited laughter. It was a bold move even from him. Luckily Lady Durrell did not take offense:

"See?" she said to Mercer, "A woman can't really afford to be nice in this world. Isn't that right, Esther?"

"Cheers to that," said Professor Franklin. "But you really could be *nicer*," she added, and they all laughed.

Elias liked Elinor the best. He'd gone through *Sense and Sensibility*, *Northanger Abbey* and *Persuasion* by now, which the Professor said was a peculiar order, but aside from *Mansfield Park*, he had not hated any of the books. Granted, *Northanger Abbey* was a bit silly, and with all the dread and poverty and self-obsessed noblemen. *Persuasion* hit a bit too close to home, but Jane Austen had overall exceeded his expectations. He had even decided to give *Mansfield Park* another go and, to his surprise, it was a different book than the one he remembered: the themes and characters were much more complex than they seemed the first time around. He could even forgive Fanny's constant pessimism— this was the future, after all, and Fanny had been right to worry.

He still thought raising money to preserve a house Jane Austen once lived in was a shallow endeavour, but he understood why those posh souls who'd never experienced real life were so determined to save it.

One sunny afternoon, when it was only he and Mabel Durrell checking for structural liabilities on the south side of Chawton Manor, they suddenly found themselves, most extraordinarily, both in a mildly cheerful mood.

"How are you liking *Emma*?" asked Lady Durrell.

"I like it."

"Really?" she seemed surprised, "How so?"

"I like that she's not exactly a good person."

She looked disappointed, which was surprisingly disappointing to him.

"You don't think Emma's a *good person*?"

The scorn on her face suggested this was not the right answer. Of course, thought Elias. She related to the spoiled heiress—and now when he pictured the character of Emma Woodhouse, previously played in his head by the drawing on the cover, she had been replaced by the righteous owner of the part, Mabel Durrell shooing her understudy to take centre stage.

"She tries to be. Everybody's trying to be good," conceded Elias.

"But she doesn't pass your little moral test."

"Which test?"

"Oh, please, Major. You must admit that, for a man devoid of belief, you are awfully judgemental."

He considered contesting these accusations, but found no compelling argument against them. So he simply asked:

"Of what do you believe me to be judgemental?"

"People who believe in things. That is what circumvents the contradiction: you believe in not believing. But, not content with that, you must roll your eyes at those who still have a cause."

Elias accidentally chuckled, which Mabel unfortunately understood. He had no choice but to verbalise it:

"And what have *you* decided to believe in? Jane Austen?"

"Art. Literature. I am in no trouble however because it teaches me no lessons, all it does is ask questions—to me that seems an improvement towards religion. I think we should put our brains to work and make sense of things by ourselves."

Thinking for yourself. What a wild idea, thought Elias.

"What use is it thinking for yourself if your actions are controlled by others?"

She stopped for a moment, unsure of the answer—then she shrugged:

"The latter is a consequence of not doing the former."

"I wish everything were as simple as you make it out to be from your high tower, Lady Durrell."

That might have been a bit too combative, but by now he had realised Mabel Durrell's favourite pastime was arguing.

"My high tower is the same as yours. Look at me, Major McBride. I'm right next to you."

Yes, thought Elias. Proud. Through no fault of my own, but still.

She cleared her throat and brought her hands together. "Since you have delivered your judgement of me, it seems fair for me to deliver my judgement of you," she declared, as if she had not been doing that from the moment they met.

"Well, let's have it, then," he decided to play along. Whatever this woman's verdict on his person, he was sure it would be both wrong and hilarious.

"You believe happiness to be a state of moral neglect."

"I thought I didn't believe in anything at all?"

"Pay attention," she reprimanded him like a schoolteacher. "You pretend not to believe in anything, but you in fact believe in nothing. You, sir, are a hypocrite."

She spoke teasingly, in a playful voice, though Elias saw it as a way to soften the blow of what she must have conceived as a difficult revelation to him.

He still laughed. What she said made a sort of unprompted sense, delightfully mistaken, sure—though at the same time it excited great curiosity in him. With a certain amount of embarrassment Elias could admit that he loved to hear people talk about him, much more than he liked to talk about himself, or others. And there was something in Lady Durrell's commanding tone that gave him a momentary sense of permanence, as if things were indeed as she saw them, even if he knew them not to be. It seemed mildly transgressive to his good sense that he should lend his ear to her nonsensical posh laments, but there was a sense of rhythm, of movement in them. So he listened to her judgement of him.

"You, Major, are a modern moralist. And those are the worst, because the poor religious moralists actually believe in having a moral code," she concluded.

"I'm sorry, Professor, but you are off the mark there. I've thought much about what life has to offer, and I am neither a nihilist nor a moralist. I am simply a realist."

"If you were as you say, you'd have no problem with the perversity of this world, the perversity of who we are and why, the bare truth and dryness of all things and people, the fact that things last longer than people. That everybody dies, in the end; everybody will."

Here was this woman, who had never seen death in her life, telling him it was pointless to put up a fight with the world because, well, people were both naturally perishable and evil. Or at least that was how he heard it. Such an outrage brewed inside him that he considered perhaps she had been right about him after all: he did have a problem accepting "perversity" as part of the human condition—if that turned him into a moralist, he didn't mind.

The war hadn't really started to get to Lady Corey's nerves until she was bitterly informed that the market was out of bananas. Fine, she'd said; then go to a different market.

"No, Lady Corey, it's not just that market that is out. The whole *country* is out of bananas."

"The whole *country*?"

"Even Scotland, Ma'am."

This was the moment Arabella decided that the war was getting out of hand.

"We should just have stayed in the neutral side of things," she said, which was neither correct nor wise: Professor Franklin took it upon herself to inform her of every social-political problem one was currently against—Arabella, whose bringing-up had prepared her to withstand disasters as great as a morbidly obese pony, did not take it well. But, much like Penny the Pony, she was rising up to the challenges of her current state.

Her spot on the Chawton team was earned in multiple fundraisers she had hosted. Besides, no one else on the team was so beautiful and captivating. Though Mabel could have perhaps been a contender in terms of looks, her acidic temperament and the fact that she never smiled had gained her a bad reputation. In true Austen spirit, one might say Mabel had both the sense and the sensibility, yet could not master the art of persuasion.

Needless to say, Arabella's epicurean placidity in all matters irritated Mabel to an extreme—and she would have perhaps long dispensed her friendship had it not been that they had known one another since birth. Not to mention that, because of the obvious nature of some of Arabella's assessments, they were quite fun to laugh at.

"Say, Arabella," Mabel said one day, "I've been thinking about Chawton. Do you think our energies would be better spent elsewhere?"

"How so?"

"I don't know. If we raised money to protect a building of historical importance, then why can't we protect people, too?"

"Because the money is for the building."

"Yes, but one can get more money for other investments."

"Protecting people is the duty of our government."

"Yes, you make a good point. The government should not privatise security. If we help one place, we'd have to help everyone else. Because, if we helped one place, public services could assume that they need not invest if we are already."

"It would be nice if everyone had the money to keep safe."

"Don't say that in public, Arabella."

"Why not?"

"That's Communist ideology."

"*That* is communism? Common sense?"

"You'd be surprised."

"Are they not our allies, though, Mabel?"

"It's nice to see you are keeping up."

"Of course I am. By the by, have you yet convinced the Major that Austen is worth saving?"

"By the by? That hardly has to do with anything."

"It had to do with what we were talking about before—you know, who we can and cannot help."

"I don't know that we can help him. He's very set in his ways."

"So are you."

"Well, sure, but my ways are the right ways," Mabel joked.

Arabella did not catch the humor. "Oh, I have been re-reading *Emma*," she said.

"Do you like it better?"

"I've always liked it."

The only book Arabella had ever read which she had not enjoyed had been *Moby Dick*—there was no reason why one should write so many pages about one bloody whale.

"Do you still think Emma and Knightley's marriage is a good idea?"

"Why do you hate Knightley so much?"

"I do not hate Knightley . . . as a reproachful uncle figure."

Arabella smiled. "It is quite odd, I admit it. But such were the times. My grandparents married when she was nineteen and he was fifty," she said.

"This is older than your grandparents."

"Older than my grandmother, perhaps."

Mabel would not press her on this—Arabella was very touchy about genealogy. Instead she proceeded:

"It's not just that Knightley is too old for Emma . . . It's that he knew her as a child. Not to mention that he scolds her like a child. And what is his business with Mr. Woodhouse anyway? How are they even friends, when one is so silly and the other so grave in aspect?"

"I don't think Knightley's intentions are necessarily malevolent," Lady Corey said, sipping her tea. As long as there was tea, she would remain strong, she had decided after the banana incident.

"I just think it's a bit icky," said Mabel. Arabella was the only person with whom she could have ventured to employ such a word. It was a slang word that was only acceptable in the context of casual friendship, and even then it must be used ironically. Arabella chuckled at the uncanny word coming out of Mabel's mouth, then said:

"Certainly. Would you ever marry a man twice your age?"

"God, no. I think Dr. Freud has said enough on that already."

"You haven't touched your tea, Mabel," said Lady Corey, whose disposition was kept afloat solely by her dwindling tea stock.

Mabel grabbed her teacup and drank dutifully, realising her dear friend was on edge, at least until the next shipment from India.

"I think I could, if I were deeply in love," said Arabella, to Mabel's confusion. "Marry a man twice my age," she clarified.

"Oh, Arabella. You aren't the type to be deeply in love. None of us are."

"Why should you think that?"

"You have too placid a temperament. But Austen is not about love."

"*Pride and Prejudice* is."

"It is about marrying above one's class."

"If you see things through Mrs. Bennet's perspective, then yes, it is about class."

"Touché," said Mabel. Perhaps there was still some potential in her friend, she thought.

There was nothing that Mabel Durrell feared more than being a product of her time. No suggestion was as disparaging to her as that of a human being belonging not to oneself, but rather to one's era. She could not tolerate the idea that she, who above all else searched for truth, was completely artificial.

In the same way, Mabel needed to think others are who they are not because of their historical conditions, but in spite of them; essentially that was their *essence*.

At university many of her students looked at her as an arrogant aesthete, concerned only with beauty and fictional places. But Beauty concerned Mabel because Beauty was Truth—and Truth should concern every human being. Beauty was not about following a given standard; it was about what was left of it once the standard was subtracted.

Of course beauty could also be made of horrid things. Many have said that truth is ugly and that art and fiction are necessary especially because they are unreal. It is not because something is unreal, however, that this something cannot be true.

Were that the case, reality would have to be true all the time—and she knew that to be a lie. Nothing is as easily manipulated as reality, because people understand it as a stand-in for fact and truth. Reality nonetheless happens for a second and then it is reborn in an endless series of differing shapes through the telling and re-telling, the eternity of interpretations. Reality is sacrificed always to that which is sly and mischievous and worst of all, liquid.

Mabel did not much care to be told what to think by others. She believed people should think for themselves—not in a "being allowed" to think for themselves way. It was more of a "people should be forced to think for themselves given the atrophied state of their inert brain cells which will only leap into action when they absolutely have to" situation. Ergo, in order to get people to think for themselves they had, first, to be told what to think by Mabel herself. That was fine, of course, because she was certain that she was absolutely unbiased.

Mabel wondered whether people had all been born incredibly stupid or whether they had just become stupid. Perhaps they just couldn't take it anymore and have given themselves a metaphorical lobotomy (Mabel understood the appeal).

She reprimanded herself; she was just very angry—positively so, because "very" is a very lazy adverb. "Angry" is a lazy adjective as well—she was, actually, furious with herself. She felt bad for feeling bad about the enemy's buildings. Perhaps Major McBride had been right, and her priorities should be those of everyone else's—but Major McBride, for all his talk, had scarcely changed anything with this attitude. She was of the opinion, however, that she had managed to change quite a bit.

Overseeing the business at Chawton Manor involved dealing with a thousand bureaucracies all at once. Elias hated that, although at least it kept his head busy. The fact that the construction work had already started was also a plus, since that meant less time spent with the Posh Posse and more with the nice enough troop whose members were deemed unqualified for fighting—women, elderly men, all trying to make ends meet.

Of course, he had to constantly remind everyone not to paint over the walls, or fix anything that had been broken for a historically relevant amount of time. There was one particular doorknob that had to be unfixed thrice until someone screwed a warning to the door: "Do not fix the damn doorknob". It was too late to save the door from this inscrutability, and it was determined that the mark left by the screw was actually a historical one—or would, at least, one day become historically relevant.

During the time spent on renovation, Elias's phantom limb problem got somewhat worse.

This is why Mrs. Joanna Barton, who worked the night shifts at the town hospital and helped with the Chawton Renovation in the afternoon, noticed that something strange was going on. One did not have to be a nurse in order to notice a bionic leg—still, Major McBride's contorted expressions and compulsive stroking of what was, essentially, wood, left her intrigued. When she took the liberty to ask him about it, he dodged her question:

"It's hard to stand on a wooden leg all day," he said.

"I know, sir. I've treated many men like you at the hospital."

"Men like me. That is tactful."

"Oh, sir, I don't mean . . . All I mean to say is that I understand."

"Of course."

"And ask whether . . . Whether you have someone to care for you."

"Care for me? I'm not an invalid in any way, Mrs. Barton!"

"I don't mean a nurse. Just someone with whom to talk."

"Talk about what?"

But she did not get a chance to finish, as Mabel had just then arrived bearing many forms and papers. She did not say good morning to any of the thirty people in the room, and instead went straight to Elias.

"I need this dispatched as soon as possible. I left some things for you to fill, like the names of the workers, etc."

"Uhm, Professor, this is Mrs. Barton."

Mabel looked up from her forms, then down at the nurse: "Yes, sure."

Then, as both Elias and Mrs. Barton stared at her, she asked, "Can I help you with something?"

"No, ma'am," said Mrs. Barton, leaving.

"You know, Professor, there is such a thing as manners. There's this marvellous book, Debrett's, perhaps you'd benefit from reading it."

Mabel pretended to laugh.

"Do you think we should use concrete or reinforced concrete for the kitchen?"

She rolled her eyes at the second option, which told him he should pick the first.

"You know the original has already been reformed, so there's very little to protect," she explained her position. Elias wondered how he'd ended up discussing home renovation in the middle of a war for humanity's soul.

"Why are you asking me this?"

"Arabella insists we be consistent because it's *nicer that way*," she said those last words with such scorn Elias wondered why Lady Durrell was friends with people she despised.

"I confess, I don't really have an opinion," he said.

"Well, then get one."

"People love having opinions—I wonder when facts will become as fashionable."

"Your witticisms have much improved, Major McBride."

Had they? Or had he read that somewhere? It sounded like something he would have laughed at, forgotten, and unknowingly plagiarised simply to sound wittier than Lady Durrell.

"Oh, yes. Thank you so much, Lady Durrell, for allowing me to achieve the maximum of insolent behaviour. Were it not for your constant demonstration of such, my potential for irritation would have gone entirely to waste."

"Well, I mean, I'm sure you'd have found it somewhere else . . ."

"Wouldn't be the same."

"Then you should demonstrate your gratitude by voting in favour of regular concrete."

"Lady Durrell, don't take this the wrong way, but that makes no difference to me or anyone but you and Lady Corey."

"Actually, it does, because the money we could save by excluding the kitchen from the plan would probably go to what you would consider worthier causes."

Such as what? Protecting Charlotte Bronte's bungalow? He wanted to ask as they made their way to the anachronistic kitchen. She sat down and poured herself some tea.

"Fine, you may report to Lady Corey that I agree with you," Elias was tired of debating concrete. He sat down, too.

"What a marvellous conclusion," Lady Durrell smiled.

"I certainly hope they will not bomb us at teatime," he looked around. "Is there enough here for all the workers?"

"How should I know? The workers are your responsibility," Mabel added milk and stirred. "What was that nurse telling you anyway? You looked like a ghost just then."

"Aren't we all ghosts?" he joked.

"No. What a ridiculous thing to say."

"I thought you spent your life going after ghosts. Trying to catch them in the palm of your hand and keep them in your private collection."

"I would never make my collection private. I think that ignorant people ought to be saved. I would donate my collection to the British Museum, which thanks to me is fortified."

"How noble of you, professor."

"Quite."

"I finished *Emma*, by the way."

"Have you really? Did you also find the ending quite poor?"

In Mabel's ideal ending, Emma would have remained single. It would have cemented the novel as Austen's masterpiece: having Emma end as the only financially independent heroine, a happy spinster who could have underscored the dilemmas of Austen's other heroines as problems primarily economic. Silly

Janeites would finally be pushed to understand that, in Austen, the struggle between love and money is resolved only when it is no longer a struggle, but a marriage.

Meanwhile, McBride was offering shallow—yet accurate—observations. "It was out of nowhere that she decided she loved Mr. Knightley. To me he seemed more like a father figure."

"Frank Churchill was better," agreed Mabel.

"But Frank Churchill was never really an option. Not to mention Austen does not make a nice case for him," said the major.

"But he is, when one thinks about it, the best of his kind as represented by Austen. In *Sense and Sensibility* there is Willoughby, who is a coward and in some ways irredeemable (though still strangely forgivable), *Mansfield Park* shows us to Henry Crawford, who is a thousand times more interesting than that bland turtle Edmund . . . Still, Austen wants us to think he's not *worthy* of Fanny. Fanny!"

Mabel's hatred of Fanny Price was intact—*not the typical Austen heroine* . . . But neither was Emma. If Mary Crawford was the livelier option for *Mansfield Park*, so was Jane Fairfax the more admirable one here. What's a typical Austen heroine anyway? Was she, Mabel, turning characters into archetypes and literature into a formula? She tried not to let this fear get in the way of what she was, still, in the process of saying:

"Even *Pride and Prejudice* . . . Oh, you haven't read it yet. My point being, from all of those inconsequential men, Frank Churchill is the only one that is let off his punishment. He gets what he wants, even if he is deemed unworthy of it."

"I guess that she thought that if Emma was getting a happy ending, it would be unfair not to give him one, too. They are really alike."

That the ending was happy is disputable, in Mabel's opinion—but she chose to respond to the claim she agreed with. "They are, aren't they? I understand the reasoning behind each marriage, but not when compared to other Austen-approved matches. In

Persuasion, for instance, Anne Elliot and Captain Wentworth seem to be just as similar in temperament as Emma and Frank."

"Emma and Frank need different people to make them better."

"But why is Anne better than Emma? Anne is a coward in many ways. She never says what she thinks, she's easily—I don't want to say *persuaded*, because, of course—manipulated. She's weak."

Mabel's own severity surprised her: she did enjoy Anne, for all her faults. Sometimes what she meant as a mere admonishment came out as an overly bombastic condemnation.

"She's better because doing nothing is better than doing something bad," suggested Elias.

"Not necessarily. Especially if one's intentions aren't bad."

"Good intentions mean nothing. Someone who does the right thing for the wrong reasons still does more than someone who means well but ends up ruining everything."

Lady Durrell considered this. "So, if one intends to wreck everything but ends up per chance doing the right thing, one is absolved," she said, as a hypothesis because she could not find an example.

"It's not a matter of absolution. None of us are absolved. We live and then we die and we're either content with our choices or not."

"One is one's own judge."

"Yes."

Mabel smiled involuntarily. "Why does that sound more dreadful than comforting?" she asked.

"Because we get to find out who we are when no one is watching, not even God."

For someone who revelled in solitude as much as she did, she was alarmingly distressed by this, like a child coming to find out her parents hadn't been watching her accomplish a somersault even though they promised to pay attention.

"The levity you bring to conversation, Major McBride!"

"One of my many talents. Or was that a rhetorical question?"

"Aren't all questions rhetorical, in a way?", she questioned, rhetorically.

"Perhaps for you," he mocked. "Do you even need me here? Or do I just make a good audience?"

"And find out who I am when no one is watching, not even God? God forbid!" Mabel dramatically threw her hands up to the sky, half-expecting to be struck by lightning.

Then there was that uncanny feeling again. She wondered whether to let him in on it. "I feel . . . somewhat of a forgery sometimes," she said.

"Well, it's probably because you always speak as though you were being quoted."

That was a good one, thought Mabel. If she'd been wearing a hat she'd have taken it off.

"Perhaps you are ready to believe no one is watching, sir—I however may need outside testimony, whether it is God or the Devil or a Soviet spy . . . I'd hate it for them to portray me in the wrong light simply because I failed to express myself properly. The radio signal could be quite poor."

"But I make such a terrible audience!"

"I've had worse," she said, which was true considering her closest friends.

"You flatter me," he said.

"Oh, I'm sorry. I didn't mean to."

"That's why I'm flattered," said Elias, thus winning the small battle of banter.

Even now, she thought, as she was hearing herself say those things, she might as well have been onstage. McBride continued with his tirade, which she must hear now, as she had encouraged it.

"But why all those speech affectations?" he asked. "You are too affected. I suppose it happens to members of the aristocracy all the time. You are always laughing at one another's witticisms, trying to beat each other at it."

"Well, I do always win, though."

"You certainly do, professor."

The ethics behind it seemed simple enough to him—Mrs. Barton's husband, despite being at the front compensating for his every sin, had been described as a raging drunk, and Mrs. Barton in her share seemed quite disposed to compensate for her previous good behaviour.

This was a dilemma for Mrs. Barton, not him. Their arrangement was easy, undemanding and well-meaning. As she herself had said, the war made everyone go a bit over the edge, and it was nice to spare oneself of a lonely moment.

Before the war Elias had had no problem being alone. He could have spent the rest of his life in the Scottish wilderness for all he cared. Isolation served him right; it enabled him to find out who he was, away from the historic condition—who he would have been in times differing from his own tragedy-riddled ones. Some would see his propensity towards solitude solely as an escape mechanism, a classic trait of avoidant personality disorder. Elias, nonetheless, simply had revelled in nature's quiet murmurs in a somewhat idealistic way; so much that now he lamented the naiveté that had propelled him to spend hours thinking about the human condition apart from place and time when that was all it was; the bloody human condition: place and time.

What the hell are artists and philosophers good for, blabbering about the essential parts of one's soul regardless of one's body, when the body is the most essential part after all? He was his body parts now; or, he was the loss of body parts.

The absence where his leg had previously been had pulled his wandering soul right back into the reality of this condition, the body, the palpable inexistence. Aren't we all just bodies after all, he thought; either alive or dead, succumbing to the will of History as a group, not individuals? Aren't men little more than lambs offered in sacrifice to a greater narrative?

Before the war he hadn't been escaping. Isolation then was not about hiding; it was about peaceful introspection. Hours wasted away, now. Now he didn't want to be alone; it hurt more when he was alone; the leg, the lack of the leg.

Introspection seemed like a cruel threat. It would provide him with the sense that he was an individual again when really he was just a fraction of one—a nameless mass, and he knew that now. It would be another fantasy, another empty fiction.

Elias' natural habitat of peaceful solitude had been taken over by the Germans, so he fled somewhere else. And yet now he was constantly fleeing, following the tides of history, and the tides of history were an ever-expanding flood.

Consequently, Elias had resigned himself to life without introspection, and could not have estimated the size of the gap forming in his gut, growing inside him like a cancer.

But how does one quantify absence? Elias could understand it only as long as he noticed it, and he had forbidden himself to search for explanations, especially for things that aren't there. He would focus on fixing things that exist, instead.

Nevertheless, as he debated the decision with himself, Mabel Durrell's snooty voice kept ringing in his head: "You pretend not to believe in anything, but you in fact believe in nothing".

It had seemed nonsensical at the time, but the more he thought about it (involuntarily), the more logical it became. Yes, because nothing *is*, and it is anything that is not. Nothing is a positive negative, and should therefore be seen as an entity in and of itself. When we say there is nothing, we acknowledge "Nothing" as a space of unknown content, but of definite existence: as a something. In conclusion, the presence of absence is a presence nonetheless.

Was that it? Was there solace to be found in this unusual interpretation? Or was he making waves out of syntax, slowly losing his mind to grammatical loopholes? As those questions accumulated and taunted his sanity, he shook them off to disperse them.

Best not to think of anything at all but the matter at hand.

Unlike our brooding major, Mabel was not yet ready to give up on her sense of self—or her sense of what other things should be—simply because of the historical conditions at play. She had already compromised, despite—and perhaps because of—Mr. Mercer's protests.

Unlike Mr. Mercer, she was less preoccupied with the building itself than with what the building meant, what it stood for. They might not have won the war yet, but this was a small battle in which she had triumphed. At least one small piece of culture would still be standing. And it may not matter now or in another ten or twenty years; but she knew at some point people would care more about this than they did about some mid-20th-century war.

Does anyone remember, after all, under which circumstances the Library of Alexandria burned to the ground, along with all the knowledge in the world? People remember only that it burned; by whom and for what doesn't matter anymore. Everyone knows the Hanging Gardens of Babylon were raised by Nebuchadnezzar, but no one knows who put them back down—just that, seeing as they are not there right now, someone did.

And, while Mabel felt very much for the citizens of Alexandria whose lives were inconvenienced due to the Siege of the city by Julius Caesar in 48 BC, she grieved not them but the loss of the Library. That was why she was raising money now to protect Oxford, Cambridge, Warwick, Stratford, and Hampton-Court and all relevant places that could lose centuries of preserved history over this war.

Germany had already been destroyed. A friend of Mr. Mercer's, fighting at the front, had sent him a letter detailing the lamentable condition of historical cities. Unfortunately he had also detailed the next planned attacks, which caused the Army to send him to prison for sharing privileged information with civilians. The letter had not been intercepted—though it could have been, or so was the reasoning of Mr. Mercer as he turned his friend in.

West German towns in particular had been ravaged. Mabel didn't feel badly for the Germans at all, but she did feel badly about the buildings. Hanover, Munster, Boon, Ingolstadt, Aachen, Heidelberg and Freiburg and Frankfurt; all over the country, those places were destroyed. Well, that must mean we are finally winning the war, she thought.

She had so many pleasant memories associated with those places, however, that she was devastated; the Germans did not deserve them. Before all this nonsense she had spent weekends there with her family; everything was so cheap in Germany, before. She knew things were cheap because of the previous war and how poor it made them. It made everyone poor but the Americans. The Americans love these wars; everyone needs to borrow money from them afterwards. As long as Europe was in ruins, Americans were fine.

After this war was over, they would do what they had done last time: devise a reconstruction plan. They like destroying things, the Americans, so they could loan money for fixing them afterwards. On that score, of course, they wouldn't worry. The oldest buildings in America were probably younger than the trees sitting next to them.

At Chawton, they were going about their work room by room. While a room was being renovated, the furniture was moved to a different one. That day, however, it just so happened that the main hall's furniture would not pass through the narrow doors of the suites and offices, and the movers had to take the historical furniture outside.

In spite of the fine weather, Elias had worried Lady Durrell would seethe over the decision, for which he decided he would take full responsibility. That is why it was so strange to come across her lying on the Victorian sofa, enjoying both the sun and a copy of *Northanger Abbey*.

Somehow Elias was more chafed by that image than he would have been had she thrown a fit about the furniture's location.

"I thought historical objects were sacred to you, Lady Durrell?" he asked as he approached her.

"They are."

"Then why are you damaging them?"

She raised her eyebrows and sat up, impressed by his boldness.

"This sofa is younger than my grandfather," she justified. "It's hardly a century old."

"Then no doubt you should allow the workers and servants to use it as well," he said, trying not to sound as annoyed as he was: the people working at Chawton had been told to sit on the floor, as their modern buttocks might cause damage to the ancient upholstery. But now it seemed that Lady Durrell's rules applied only to everyone else.

"You have got yourself a point," she admitted, promptly rising from the couch. "When I said that, I meant only the original furniture. I never would have thought you'd interpret it as everything. Where have you even been sitting? Sit down, please, Major McBride. I'm sure, with your leg . . ."

"I'm fine, thank you," he interrupted. Lady Durrell's reaction was obviously to blame someone else for her shortcomings.

There was no use pointing that out, though, as she had already started a different subject.

"By the way, I've been thinking, Major, that the least I could do after this house is ready is to make it available as a bomb shelter. That way the people are protected as well. Two birds, one stone and all that."

She looked rather happy with herself for doing the bare minimum.

"That is very generous of you, Ma'am."

"Don't make a mockery out of flattery—I take it very seriously, mind you. It's why I keep Mr. Mercer around."

"Oh, that's why."

"Indeed. He's like one of those American pep-rally girls, a cheerleader. *You're doing great, Lady Durrell! Splendid! What a remarkable person you are, Lady Durrell!* God, he's like an intensely positive gnat flying around, giving me a constant buzz of hurrah."

To everyone else, he is just a gnat, thought Elias. At least he extended Elias the common courtesy of only coming on weekends, whereas Lady Durrell was here every day.

"And Professor Franklin?"

"What about her?"

"Why do you keep her around?"

"Oh, she's a serious person. It's possible to have an actual conversation with her. Every conversation feels dispensable these days. People are like moths circling around a lamp, afraid of the lamp. They always want to talk of the war without ever thinking about the war."

Another insect metaphor—that's what you get from an aristocrat in a garden.

"You know, ma'am, you could do *something*," said Elias, as in something useful, he meant. "On top of this, I mean."

"What? I'm useless with fuses, so I can't be a mechanic or electrician, I am a terrible driver, I am nauseated by blood . . . The things that I know . . . I know of abstract things."

"I'm sure you could learn how to operate a machine, or dispatch a telegram," he suggested.

"Well, anyone can do *that*."

"Exactly," said Elias, although he had his doubts regarding Lady Corey.

As a matter of fact, Mabel had at the start of the war enlisted herself to help, but her father found out and forbade her. Even though she was relieved about it, she'd actually wanted to go when she signed up for it, on a whim. At war, people who want to kill each other simply kill each other. One does not have to waste time decoding social rituals. You don't really have to talk, if you don't want to. There is no performance element in place.

"Well, in case you haven't heard, Major, I am a remarkable person. So, forgive me if I refuse menial work," she laughed it off.

"I can never tell when you're being serious," he said.

Neither can I, thought Mabel.

"I think you're being serious," continued the major, "but then you smile to pretend you're joking. But you *actually* think you're above menial work."

"Well, that is why people go to university."

"People go to university because they are rich. It has nothing to do with dignity. Look at Mr. Mercer."

"I thought you believed everyone had a right to good education," she said.

"What good it all is! You're spending millions on a hobby while half the country starves to death!"

This mightily offended Mabel, who believed that university should be not only free, but also it should be mandatory: sure, not everyone is suited for an academic life—an undergraduate course, however, would not be much of an effort.

"When the war is over and all of our buildings are still intact, Britain will thank me. They may even thank you."

"No need to thank me. I'm taking off."

"You can't. You're here on official duty!"

"Well, I'm reassigning myself, effective immediately. This is ridiculous work and you are out of touch with reality, Lady Durrell!"

Where had all this rage come from? She never expected this level of insubordination, and from a soldier at that! Good riddance, she thought, and spoke harshly, hoping to sting. "Well, go, then, give evacuation training! I don't need you, anyway; I only took you in as a favour to your Colonel. He said you'd been so anxious lately, having lost the leg and all. I took pity on you. But, if you want to go, go. We'll be fine without you."

Everything Old is New Again

Mabel had been a peculiar child, impatient to learn, and something of an outcast who spent more time debating philosophical truths with her library books than she did making friends. She did not particularly care for people, though she did enjoy dogs and horses. From a young age, she felt that most people's conversations were little more than unnecessary conjecturing; she longed for solitude above all, and after spending too long at social functions she felt positively drained.

In short, Mabel Durrell was not cut out to deal with people. Some people she of course loved and cared for—Arabella and her parents, for instance—though like all others they were always more cherished from a distance.

Strangely enough, she was a great public speaker, which made her a truly wonderful teacher—her problem really was with one-on-one conversations. Her parents had taken her to a speech therapist as a child due to her difficulty in getting through sentences Much like His Majesty the King, Mabel had stuttered. The stuttering of course disappeared when she was addressing her teacher at class or a crowd at debate club.

All in all, Mabel did care about people, albeit in the way that most people care about the rain forest: we all realise it should be protected, but we're not too fussy about it. Mabel did care greatly for humanity—she cared about the meaning of life, and the uncanny trajectory of the human race. That is why she read, rather than talked, and why she helped buildings and paintings, rather than actual human beings.

Some of us, she told herself, are born with a greater sense of purpose than others. Some of us happen to be gifted with better brains. It wasn't her fault that she was smarter than everyone. She was a remarkable person—that should more than make up for her lack of social skills. Most of the time, she was cold. That was her natural temperament; and trying to be warm overheated her, backfired, and made her sweat and feel disgusted at herself.

Mable didn't really know what would have become of her, had she been born to a less fortunate family. She might have been required to ride buses and trains on her own. She probably would have been assigned to a job that involved a great deal of conversation with mean strangers, or to a task like sewing, or putting things together—all things for which she was utterly hopeless. And then there was the question of crowded spaces; she'd heard of people having to share a bed with all their siblings; she'd seen people get suffocated inside the Metro and manage to come out alive. She felt certain that she would never survive those ordeals.

How does one cultivate a soul with such a life? There could be no individuality, just basic human cruelty and filth. If you can never be alone with your soul, never even come to understand that you had a soul, how could you even be a person? It would be impossible—a life made up only of basic animal needs, and then death.

Elias felt humiliated that even a man like Colonel Hendricks, a fussy man-child, took pity on him. After his argument with Lady Durrell, Elias went straight to see him. At first, Hendricks pretended not to know a thing about the arrangement Lady Durrell revealed. But then, when he realized that it had been exposed, he confessed rather dramatically. No sooner had he given his excuses, Elias forgave him—he didn't really want to get into any lingering unpleasantness. So, back to the bombs. Back to drills. Back to the dreary days of war that would go on forever.

He continued to read Austen, though. There wasn't much for him to do other than that. It was the most frustrating.

A full month had passed—Chawton Manor seemed near to completion—when he received a letter from one Mrs. Argent, of whom he'd never heard. Soon enough, however, he recognized her on the handwriting:

My Dear Elias,

As you can probably infer from my signature, Albie and I got married—last fall, in Glasgow. It was a lovely day in spite of the war. We saw the McKinleys, too. They seemed rather thin, but assured us they were fine.

We'll be coming down to London next September, and were wondering whether you would like to meet us. It does not do one well to spend so much of one's day brooding and rereading the papers. One can meet us and still achieve the desired amount of brooding for the day all the same.

Because the mail is lousy right now, I will tolerate a wider window for your answer. I beg you to remember your old friends in times such as these, and let yourself live a little. The war will still be there when you get back.

> *Albie and I are rather worried about you, Elias. We hope you have found yourself some friends down there—otherwise we may have to move (yes, on your account)! The very best wishes from your dear friend,*
>
> *Mrs. Meredith I. Argent*
>
> *PS: You aren't mad at Albie, are you? He is quite worried that you are.*

Oh, isn't it fantastic? Albie and Meredith had married and not even bothered to invite him—so what was this now? Acting like nothing happened? Like they're all good friends? Codswallop.

Miss Meredith, the youngest of the Misses Ingres, had grown up with him and been his fiancée for a good part of the war. Upon his return, however, she declared him unfit for happiness, or something of the sort.

"You are always in a mood! Nothing I do could possibly make you happy," she often complained. "All you do is push people away. I cannot reach you anymore. It's like you're staring at life through a veil. "

Elias, having been recently robbed of a leg, had no patience for her annoyance whatsoever. She didn't quite understand war; she didn't understand she was the one behind the veil. It was all the better she had married Albie, who could not fight on account of his terrible eyesight. Of course, to see reality as it was would shake both of them to the core. After such a shock, day-to-day life lost its plausibility.

Though he did not feel the letter dignified a response at first, he changed his mind when he realized that his indifference could be misinterpreted as resentment. Thus he settled to write the driest letter he could think of:

> *Dear Mrs. Argent,*
>
> *I am glad to hear you and Albie are well. Please assure him that I am not mad at him.*

Unfortunately, I'm afraid I won't be able to see you in September—due to official state business, I'm no longer staying in London and it would be quite impossible for me to get out of this most urgent matter of fortifying historical buildings, with which I am currently involved.

All the best,
Major Elias McBride

When Elias showed up at Chawton, Lady Durrell grinned so uncomfortably that he almost turned back. It had been a game in her mind, and his presence meant he had caved.

"Oh, Major McBride! I was starting to wonder when you'd come apologise and beg me to give back your job."

"Apologise for what?"

Once again, she was delightfully overdressed, holding a spreadsheet in one hand and having the other hold the hem of her dress.

"Lucky for you I am willing to let bygones be bygones."

"Professor Durrell," he said. "I'm here about the bomb shelter. You said we could inspect it, make sure it has everything it needs."

The truth was that he could have sent somebody else, but didn't want what he had written in the reply to Meredith to be a complete lie.

"Yes, someone is, at the moment, digging a hole in my garden. I couldn't let them destroy the original floors, so we'll have a secret passage into the kitchen, which as you know has already been renovated in the Victorian Era. Mr. Mercer says having it changed compromises historical integrity, but I hardly think that to be the case—I actually think it makes Chawton even more thrilling."

In his absence, the "Sitting Ban" had been lifted. The Major understood that Lady Durrell was now all right with common people using the furniture because she was under the delusion that what they were doing in Chawton could be categorised as a relevant part of the people's history. If that sort of bizarre reasoning was what led her to allow alterations to the building, though, he would neither judge nor mock.

She went on fantasizing: "I can imagine dozens of tourists coming here, fifty years from now, in awe of every aspect of the house and the historical relevance of it all. We really are creating a living history here."

Yes, Professor Durrell looked rather pleased with herself. Elias had been expecting violent reprimands, but she seemed to have forgotten all about their argument. Perhaps his words hadn't been as harmful to her as hers had been to him.

"All right. Glad to see everything's at work here, Lady Durrell. I'll go check on the construction men, then."

Her hands made an absent-minded gesture, signalling off-you-go-then, and once again he felt part of his pride carelessly wounded.

Elias wanted to live inside a Jane Austen novel. The world was much simpler then. Nothing happened but spats. One had carriages and horses, and really didn't ever have to go to London.

In any case, those were the sort of dreams he had; either frivolous dreams or dreams of frivolity. He hated himself most of the time—or rather he hated himself for not hating himself. He was tired and he wondered why he had to live at this turn in history, when everything was horrid all the time, on a major scale. He could tolerate things being horrible on a minor scale, even if they were horrible all the time. For instance, it must have been terrible to live during the Black Plague, but the Plague hadn't been something that happened because a couple of idiots got together and thought it was a good idea. He'd definitely rather die or suffer over random tragedies than over one which was a deliberate choice.

He hadn't thought about what he would do once the war was over.

The hope for victory was looking better now, but he wouldn't count the chickens before they hatched. Still, it couldn't last much longer on either side. Unless the Germans or Japanese wanted to bomb the Americans, things couldn't continue as they were. And as for bombing the Americans—good luck doing that—there is a reason why they have been relatively unscathed. It is too easy, really, when there is a whole ocean between oneself and the enemy. Sure, there had been an attack on Pearl Harbour, but Elias suspected it might have been staged. The Americans needed an excuse to get in on this war, and the Japanese could not have been so stupid as to give one to them on a silver platter.

When he shared that thought with Colonel Hendricks, however, the state of his mental health was questioned—which in itself was contradictory, since no one in the country could possibly vouch for sanity at the moment, and those able to stay calm were probably mad.

Chawton was beautifully coming together. It did make him happy; to think that building would stand the war, that at least one thing would remain itself. The people obviously wouldn't, even if they survived, they would survive without living or thriving, the same way he did.

It wasn't about the leg. Of course he would take it back if given the chance—but it happened before the leg, in a way. He'd seen it happen to those soldiers who had fought the Great War; they were so deeply traumatised, so irreparably damaged, that they became numb.

Those soldiers were the ones who spent months in trenches, along with the rats and the dead and the blood.

No one was allowed to leave the trenches and the trenches filled up with cadavers going through varying stages of decomposition. But, from the start, wasn't it just a body anyway? The greatest loss was dignity and these men had lost that the day they went inside this underworld. From then on, they could only expect decay; it had already started within them.

Elias hadn't been forced to sit in the defecation of other people, or feed on rats to survive, but he felt that might as well have happened. It hadn't taken all that in order to break him—fear and physical pain and powerlessness had served him just as well.

Yes, Elias had lost his dignity. Yet, what "dignity" was he could not define; he simply could tell it wasn't there.

On the second of May, the War ended in Europe. Lady Corey, whose pantry was almost out of tea, sprang up to her feet and exclaimed "Wheee!" Professor Franklin declared to the St. Augustine's board that she would not be moving to America after all. Mr. Mercer, in the most frantic of moods, showed up at Lady Durrell's house and asked her to marry him. Mabel, whose spirits were already high, had the biggest laugh of her life.

"Mr. Mercer, I don't think we're quite suited for each other," she explained, on the verge of snorting.

"But we are in love, my dearest Mabel! I know you feel the way I feel! What we have, the . . . what do they call it? Banter! Our romance is based on banter. For once, though, be honest with me. Be honest with yourself. Listen to your heart," begged Mr. Mercer, throwing himself at her feet.

Mabel feigned solemnity, touching the left side of her chest with one hand and pressing her ear with the other.

"I'm listening to it . . . It's saying *no, no, no, no, no, no, no.*"

"But Mabel . . ."

She rang the bell for the housekeeper.

"Yes, just a minute, Mr. Mercer," she started, but she could no longer contain her laughter, "Hello, Mrs. Gray. You will not believe the audacity of this man. Tell her what you just told me."

"Mrs. Gray, I asked Lady Durrell here to marry me."

Mrs. Gray looked over to Mabel for permission to react. When she was given that, she chuckled heartily.

"Could you please call my parents, Mrs. Gray? They will certainly be amused by this."

"Of course, Lady Durrell," Mrs. Gray said, and left.

"Why must you humiliate me, Mabel?"

"You have humiliated yourself," she replied, walking over to the telephone to tell Arabella what had just happened:

"Mr. Mercer, Lady Corey wants to speak with you," said Mabel, passing him the receiver.

"Yes, hello, Lady Corey, Mr. Mercer speaking."

"Mabel tells me you asked for her hand in marriage. Certainly that cannot be true?"

"It was a practical joke that got out of hand, really," he decided. "The point is that I am so happy the war has ended, I feel like I can do anything," he forced a laugh.

"Oh, that explains it," said Lady Corey. "What a comedian you are, Mr. Mercer."

"Yeah, well . . ."

Thus Mr. Mercer was allowed to bow out of his pursuit with his dignity, and soon enough even he was convinced it had all been a brilliant practical joke.

Mabel stared fixedly at the painting of a landscape. It had been stolen by the Nazis from a prominent Jewish family, and now that the war was over it must be returned to its rightful owners. Mabel's job in the MFAA was to match works of art stolen in the Nazi plunder with their rightful owners—a remarkably difficult task, as those alive were difficult to trace, and record of provenance had been erased by the thieves.

She was rambling to herself.

"We go to museums so they'll take us somewhere else. But it's the strangest thing; that looking at a painting of a landscape is more moving than looking at the landscape itself. So much so that, if I were equidistant to the landscape and the museum, I would rather visit the painting."

Elias looked at Mabel who looked at the painting. He had been momentarily irritated by her use of the word *equidistant*, but decided to let it go, and Mabel kept going:

"You know, I have actually been to this place," she said. "It's in the Alps—awe-inspiring, really. Almost too much for the naked eye, like you would need a filter."

"Well, there you have it," said Elias, to whom landscape painting was only one step above still life as the dullest artform. Lady Durrell, as usual, was staring at it thinking not about what was in front of her, but about what it meant.

"You look at the painting and long for the landscape, but you look at the landscape and long for the painting. Bring one to the other? It wouldn't make a difference. They're entirely different places. The painting is the promise of a place that the actual place does not keep. The painter stole the landscape's spirit away and locked it between these frames. Perhaps that's what the natives meant went they prohibited cameras and said that cameras stole a person's soul away."

"That makes sense," Elias said, because it did. He didn't like to have his photo taken, either. The last time he let himself be photographed was when the work at Chawton Manor was completed, and even then it was a group photograph: Elias, Professor Franklin, Lady Corey, Lady Durrell, and Mr. Mercer.

"At some point the things are just symbols standing for memories," said Mabel, wistfully. "I don't know who we are without this . . . constant remembrance of ourselves and the individuals we represent; as long as we represent ourselves. I don't know if we are anything but."

"We have to be," said Elias. "You can still recover the memory of the thing and so at some point all things are memories of themselves."

"And so are people; telling ourselves who we are over and over," Mabel agreed.

"What do you tell yourself you are?" he asked.

"Many wonderful things. After all, it's not just me telling myself who I am: I am also being told, by others—for instance, this morning you called me a proper snob; I need to balance that out by giving myself compliments," said Lady Durrell.

"Of course, but I didn't mean to offend you. A *proper* snob, I said! An improper snob would have been much worse."

"That's true, I have earned my arrogance, no doubt. You on the other hand have hardly earned your petulance," she scolded.

"It comes with the job," he turned to stare at a painting of men riding horses.

The job in question was that of Lady Durrell's personal assistant. That he would not only accept it, but also enjoy it, was still confounding to Elias. But this was important work, finally. This was socially-engaged work, and he was glad to see people reunited with their art—people who had suffered much more than him, brought to tears by the sight of a Vermeer. He also remembered the same happening to Mr. Mercer when the MFAA told him he must return half of his rare book collection as it had been bought from duplicitous sellers. Mr. Mercer promptly (and unsuccessfully) claimed his books were forgeries and that he, too, had been swindled by the thieves.

"I can think of a couple descriptions in our references that match this painting, but it might be a forgery. I really hope it isn't. I'll call Lowell so he can verify it," she said and sighed.

Mabel's nose was one millimetre from the top of a mountain, or the symbol of a mountain, or the copy of the symbol of a mountain.

"All things and people are repetitions of themselves, trying to recover who they were, filling us in on our pasts," she was rambling again.

They had already started rebuilding the richest, most central parts of German cities. Walking up and down some streets, you couldn't even tell none of those buildings were real—true.

They were real in the sense that they were not fictional; they just weren't the true buildings.

The discrepancy between reality and truth had never been as great as it had been in Nazi Germany, thought Mabel. She wished she didn't know about the reconstructions (amongst other things).

Things are memories of themselves. Aren't they? Didn't it matter whether a painting was true or false? Doubtlessly, it was real—she had reminded Elias of the necessary distinction about seven times since they had arrived in Germany. Forgeries, forgeries, forgeries. Forgeries of buildings in Münster; special plaques to the ones that survived. *This building was not bombed in the Second World War and remains held by the same materials which held it in the year of its construction, 1232.* Plaques like this had been commissioned by the dozens; but Mabel didn't understand— if they wanted to reconstruct everything exactly as it was, then why break this pleasant delusion by revealing the true survivors? Of course the buildings must be reconstructed—anything else would have changed everything about Europe. Of course everything was already changed in Europe. Mabel meant about the Europe that came before; the Europe she cherished to wander through, that of the inconsolable.

Her consolation was the human body—she had recently read that every cell in our bodies was renewed every seven years. That did not mean that we were not still ourselves. Or did it? She had no memory of what she'd just said, though it sounded so smart when she said it. She thought she did mean the fact that we existed in constant remembrance was good—perhaps we were even more ourselves the more we remembered. Perhaps these buildings and houses were more themselves, were *asserting* themselves; by being reminded of themselves? It sounded way too complicated. She couldn't look at them without thinking about it. She decided to look at them without thinking about it. One day humans will successfully exterminate themselves and the Earth shall have no memory of our existence, she thought while looking at the renovated houses. So at some point none of this will have been real—it will have been true, but not exactly real. Earth is too big for reality. Reality is the opposite of fiction, not falseness. Reality and fiction are complementary worlds and memory is the line between them.

Truth, Earth, Falsehood, Evidence; those are all objective things. Reality and the world and fiction and memories; those suit us better. But the truth is that reality cannot be found without memory and memory does not exist exempt of fiction and fiction is irrelevant if not true.

Mabel had always wondered why it was that she would always rather experience things vicariously. They just felt more real. Perhaps it was that they felt truer. They were in the realm of the soul, and not that of the body. She had tried to convince Elias of that after the war—he was doing a bit better.

They were an odd pair, those two—theirs was a strange friendship. Whether it ever evolved into more than that, it isn't for us to know—this isn't a Jane Austen novel.